For Ann, for all the places we've been. Where shall we go next?
—C. T.

For Banjo Al—not an Al-paca, but just as sweet.
—E. C.

BEACH LANE BOOKS
An imprint of Simon & Schuster Children's Publishing Division
1230 Avenue of the Americas, New York, New York 10020
Text © 2025 by Carrie Tillotson
Illustration © 2025 by Elisa Chavarri
For information about special discounts for bulk purchases, please contact Simon & Schuster Special Sales
at 1-866-506-1949 or business@simonandschuster.com.
The Simon & Schuster Speakers Bureau can bring authors to your live event. For more information or to book an event,
contact the Simon & Schuster Speakers Bureau at 1-866-248-3049 or visit our website at www.simonspeakers.com.
Book design by Greg Stadnyk
The text for this book was set in Pleuf and Brandon.
The illustrations for this book were rendered in acrylic gouache.
Manufactured in China
1024 SCP
First Edition
2 4 6 8 10 9 7 5 3 1
Library of Congress Cataloging-in-Publication Data
Names: Tillotson, Carrie, author. | Chavarri, Elisa, illustrator.
Title: Alpacas here, alpacas there / Carrie Tillotson ; illustrated by Elisa Chavarri.
Description: First edition. | New York : Beach Lane Books, 2025. | Includes bibliographical references. | Audience: Ages 4-8 | Audience: Grades 2-3 |
Summary: "Learn all about alpacas in both North and South America in this rhyming nonfiction picture"— Provided by publisher.
Identifiers: LCCN 2024005679 (print) | LCCN 2024005680 (ebook) | ISBN 9781665942027 (hardcover) | ISBN 9781665942034 (ebook)
Subjects: LCSH: Alpaca—Juvenile literature.
Classification: LCC QL737.U54 T55 2025 (print) | LCC QL737.U54 (ebook) | DDC 599.63/67—dc23/eng/20240412
LC record available at https://lccn.loc.gov/2024005679
LC ebook record available at https://lccn.loc.gov/2024005680

Acknowledgments

The author thanks many individuals and organizations who shared their expertise throughout the research, writing, and fact-checking process of the many versions of this book, including Laurel Shouvlin, owner at Bluebird Hills Farm; Mariana Llanos, author; Max Leonard Delgado Montufar, Peruvian tourism guide; Eric Hoffman, author of *The Complete Alpaca Book*; Doug Campbell, owner at Alpacas of Oregon; Steve Johnson, owner at Paca Paradise Ranch; Quechua Benefit; Sarah Lyon, board member at Centro de Textiles Tradicionales del Cusco; Dr. Christopher Cebra, professor of camelid medicine at Oregon State University; Lona Nelsen Frank, owner at ALPACAS of Tualatin Valley, LLC; and Leanne Stoneberg, owner at Stoneberg Alpacas.

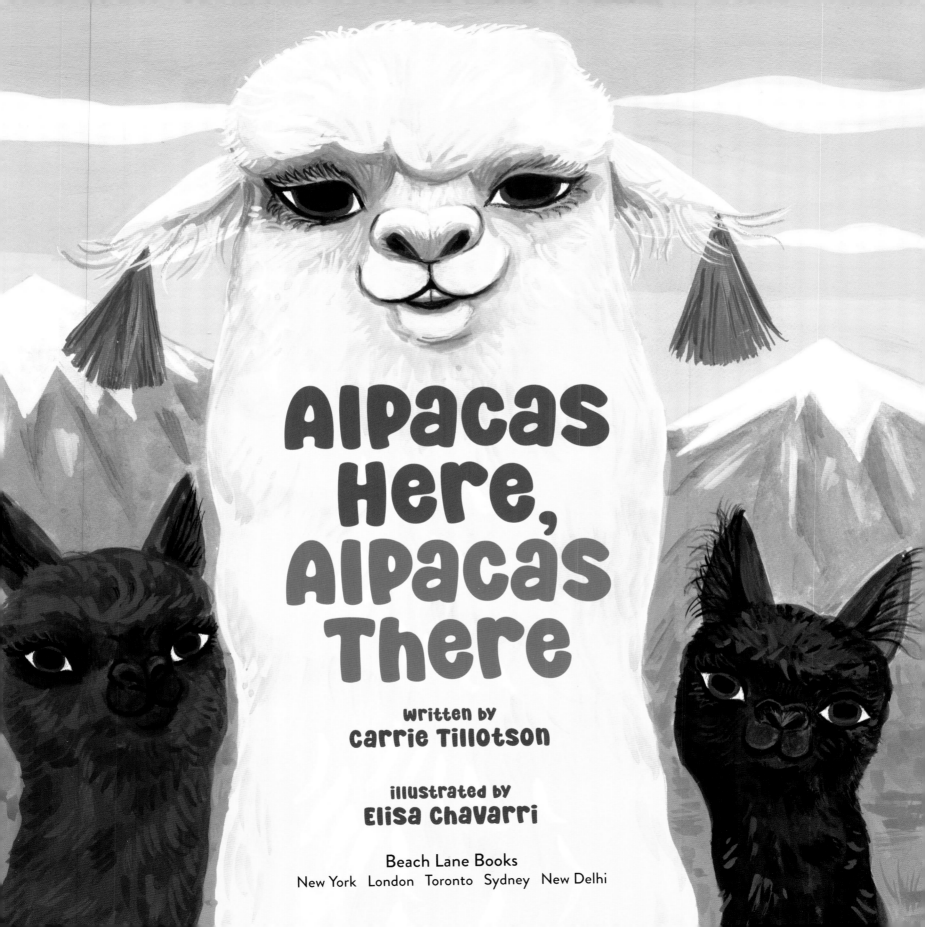

Alpacas Here, Alpacas There

written by
Carrie Tillotson

illustrated by
Elisa Chavarri

Beach Lane Books
New York London Toronto Sydney New Delhi

Beneath a brilliant
starry sky,
where mountains soar
and condors fly,

some early people
took great care
of creatures with
warm fleece to share.

Thousands of years ago, high in the Andes Mountains of South America, people domesticated alpacas from wild animals. The alpacas grew soft fleece that provided warmth in a cold climate. Today, millions of alpacas are still raised in the Andean highlands, especially in Peru. In recent years, alpaca farming has spread to North America and other places around the world. No matter where they live, alpacas everywhere share many rhythms of life. . . .

Alpacas here,
alpacas there,

relax and rest
in Mama's care.

Baby alpacas are called crias. In South America, crias are typically born from early January through March, when grass grows long and lush. In North America, they are usually born from May through September, when days grow long and warm. No matter where they live, most alpaca mothers give birth during the day so their babies can warm up and dry out before nightfall.

Among the herd,
peekaboo!

Corralled and close,
they hum and coo.

Alpaca mothers and newborns hum as a way of bonding or to find each other in a crowd. In South America, crias are often born out on the puna, the open plains of the Andean highlands. In North America, crias are usually born in pastures. Sometimes they snuggle with their mothers, separate from the herd. But not for long—alpacas are social animals and feel best when gathered in groups.

They huddle up
while night winds rush.

Beneath the rafters,
rest and hush.

Many alpacas in South America sleep in stone corrals that block gusty winds so they can keep warm. Alpacas in North America usually sleep in a three-sided shelter or barn. Wherever they rest, alpacas often snooze in a cush position, lying down with all four legs tucked underneath.

They forage through
the mountain pass.

Or nip and nibble verdant grass.

At birth, crias drink their mother's milk. Later, they munch bunches of grass scattered across the South American highlands or, in North America, graze in a pasture and eat hay in a barn.

While winter brings

its crystal shawl,

Alpaca fleece is soft and dense, like a blanket. In the majestic Andes Mountains, where snow and frost sometimes gloss the ground, fluffy fleece keeps alpacas warm.

in summer's blaze

they laze and sprawl.

In North America, where summer heat swelters, alpacas may saunter through sprinklers or lounge in a pool to keep cool.

Alpacas here,
alpacas there,

depend on people
for their care.

Today, thousands of families in the Andean highlands still depend on alpacas. The animals provide fleece for warmth and income, meat for food, and dung for fuel and fertilizing crops. There, raising alpacas is a way to survive in a place where little else thrives. But wherever they live, alpacas rely on people to protect and care for them.

Their fleece grows long.
Then, once a year,

the farmers gather . . .

Once a year, alpacas' fleece is sheared, or cut off. It's a big job that requires many skillful hands. In the Andean highlands, shearing usually happens every one to two years. In parts of North America where summers are hot, alpacas are typically sheared every year. Shearing keeps alpacas healthy so they don't overheat under the weight of too much fleece.

time to shear!

With fleece pulled tight,
hands *SNIP-snip-SNIP*.

A buzzing wand
goes *CLIP-clip-CLIP.*

Shearing is like getting a haircut. Many farmers in South America trim their alpacas' fleece with hand shears or a knife, following in the tradition of their alpaca-raising ancestors. In North America, farmers usually use electric shears.

Assorted colors
flurry, whirl!

From fleece to yarn,
they spin and twirl.

Alpaca fleece is often categorized into twenty-two colors in South America and sixteen colors in North America. Once the fleece is spun into yarn, people on both continents weave, knit, and crochet it into items like hats, blankets, ponchos, and gloves.

But hunters lurk.
They sneak and creep,

or run and chase,
and pounce and LEAP!

Many animals prey on alpacas, including Andean foxes and condors in South America and dogs, coyotes, bears, and wolves in North America. But one of alpacas' most dangerous predators—pumas, which are also called cougars or mountain lions—lives and hunts on both continents.

Jaws attack!
Sling, SMACK!

The hunters flee
and don't come back.

Alpacas need protectors, especially dogs, fences, and humans, to guard against predators in both South and North America. In South America, herders may carry a waraqa, or sling. When danger strikes, they load the waraqa with a stone, swing it overhead, and sling away!

Now safe and sound,

they pronk and prance

When alpacas pronk, they spring all four feet off the ground at once with stiff, straight legs.

through evening's glow—

a bouncing dance!

Alpacas, especially crias, often love to pronk and play at sunset, whether across the wide-open puna or fence-lined fields.

Alpacas here,
alpacas there,

grow soft and fluffy
fleece to share.

Although there is only one species of alpaca, there are two breeds—huacaya and suri. The puffy, dense fiber of huacaya alpacas crimps and crinkles, giving them a sweet, teddy bear–like look. The rarer suri alpaca's fiber hangs in long, lustrous locks. Both types of alpaca fleece are among the softest of all animal fibers, cozier and smoother to wear than sheep's wool.

They warm the hearts

and heads
and hands
of everyone . . .

across the lands.

Author's Note

I first learned about alpacas while on vacation in Washington State. My sister and I drove past a farm and wondered what the adorable, fluffy animals grazing in the pasture were. We stopped and found . . . alpacas! Ever since, I have been smitten with these gentle, charming creatures. Over the years, I've visited many alpaca farms in my area and even looked into starting my own. I soon discovered alpacas need more care, time, money, and room to roam than I had available. Later, I realized I could share my love of alpacas by writing about them. Through my research, I learned that raising alpacas is not only a way of life but a means of survival for many people in the Andes Mountains. I was drawn to the similarities in the lives alpacas lead, no matter where on Earth they live. Just like us.

Artist's Note

When I think about why I was immediately drawn to Carrie's alpaca manuscript, it was not just because alpacas are some of the most adorable, goofy, yet majestic creatures alive. Much like this book's title, I am also from here and from there. Peru is my homeland, where I was born and spent my earliest years. The States, Michigan in particular, are where I was raised, and where I now reside. Every time I see an Alpaca here, it is like seeing a little piece of Peru—it warms my heart and always makes me smile. The art in this book is heavily inspired by Peruvian folk art and use of color, which often juxtaposes very bright colors with earth tone hues. The endpaper alpacas resemble painted ceramics, while beautiful textiles and patterns, often woven out of alpaca yarn, are shown throughout. It was a joy to share the beauty of both North and South America on these pages and how these lovely creatures can thrive and contribute in each region.

More about Alpacas

Around 6,000 years ago, ancestors of Quechua and Aymara Indigenous peoples in South America domesticated alpacas. They lived high in the Andes Mountains, over 4,000 meters (13,000 feet) above sea level, in areas now known as parts of Peru, Bolivia, Chile, and Argentina. Scientists think alpacas were domesticated primarily from vicuñas, a wild relative that still lives today. Over generations of breeding, alpacas grew thicker and fluffier coats than vicuñas. Alpacas were prized for their fleece, which helped Andean people stay warm in a harsh climate. Later, cultures such as the Chiribayas and Incas developed advanced breeding programs. Archaeological evidence from naturally mummified alpacas indicates their alpacas had finer fleeces, with fibers measuring smaller in diameter, or width across, than today's alpacas. The Incas valued alpacas so much, they counted their wealth in cloth made from alpaca and vicuña fiber. Unfortunately, many Incan breeding practices were lost during the Spanish conquest 500 years ago, when invaders ravaged Incan society and destroyed South American livestock like alpacas and llamas in favor of colonial animals like horses, mules, and sheep. Yet the tradition of alpaca farming endures. For thousands of years, Andean people have passed down a culture of raising alpacas and weaving.

Today, most of the world's more than 4 million alpacas live in South America, with about 85 percent in Peru alone. Peru is the world's leading alpaca fiber producer. There, the alpaca industry is a big business, with large operations selling alpaca fleece to fashion designers around the world. But for more than 82,000 rural families, raising alpacas remains central to their survival, culture, and way of life.

Alpacas were first imported into North America in the 1980s. Early investors wanted to earn money by breeding alpacas and selling their offspring and their fleece. But the US market for alpaca fiber has been slow to take off. Although small numbers of alpacas are raised on farms across North America and in other places around the world, alpacas are increasingly championed as sustainable livestock because of the low impact they have on the environment. Unlike cattle, their soft, padded feet leave pastures undamaged, and when they eat, they cut grass with their teeth instead of pulling it up by the roots. Their three-part stomachs digest grass so efficiently that they require little additional food. Their dung makes an excellent fertilizer for gardening. Finally, unlike sheep's wool, which must be washed and stripped of a greasy substance called lanolin, alpaca fiber requires no chemical processing. This eco-friendly fleece is ready to be transformed into soft fabrics that warm people the world over. As of this writing, about 200,000 registered alpacas currently live in North America, mostly in the United States.

A Range of Alpaca-Raising Practices

Alpaca farming practices can differ across countries, regions, and communities, not just between South and North America. For instance, not all alpacas sleep in stone corrals in South America; some may sleep in covered stone structures, or even barns. And not all alpaca farms in North America have guard dogs. Throughout this book, I attempted to describe alpacas as their lives would be on different farms in each location and give a glimpse into unique and interesting practices. For example, some farmers in South America may use a waraqa to ward off predators, but guard dogs are even more common. I chose to describe many of the South American scenes among smaller family farmers in the highlands of Peru to highlight the importance of raising alpacas as a way of survival among communities living there today.

South American Camelids

Alpacas belong to a group of four animals known as South American camelids, which includes alpacas, llamas, vicuñas, and guanacos. Here's how to tell the four species apart:

alpacas: Spear-shaped ears, soft fleece, smaller and shorter than a llama, bred for their fleece, come in many colors, domesticated primarily from vicuñas.

llamas: Banana-shaped ears, generally coarser fleece, largest of the four camelids, stronger than alpacas and often used as pack animals, come in many colors, domesticated from guanacos.

vicuñas: Straight ears, one of the finest and most valuable fleeces in the world, slender, smallest of the four camelid species, typical coloring includes cinnamon-brown back and white underbelly, wild animal.

guanacos: Straight ears, coarser fleece, slightly smaller than llamas, typical coloring includes pale brown back with a white underbelly and gray face, wild animal.

South American camelids are related to Bactrian and dromedary camels.

Glossary

Andes Mountains: the tallest and longest mountain range in South America

cria: a baby alpaca

cush: when an alpaca lies down with all four legs tucked underneath

domesticated: refers to animals tamed and adapted over time from their wild counterparts for human companionship and use

fleece: an alpaca's coat of fiber, similar to hair or fur

huacaya: a type of alpaca with puffy, dense, crimped fleece

pronk: to spring all four feet off the ground at once with stiff, straight legs

puna: a high-elevation grassland of the Altiplano plateau of the Andes Mountains

suri: a type of alpaca with long, lustrous locks of fleece that hang down

waraqa: a sling to throw stones

Selected Sources

"About Alpacas." Alpacas Owners Association, Inc. (website). https://www.alpacainfo.com/academy/about-alpacas.

"Alpaca." National Geographic (website). https://www.nationalgeographic.com/animals/mammals/facts/alpaca.

"Alpaca." Smithsonian's National Zoo & Conservation Biology Institute (website). https://nationalzoo.si.edu/animals/alpaca.

Bolin, Inge. *Growing up in a Culture of Respect: Child Rearing in Highland Peru.* Austin, TX: University of Texas Press, 2006.

Callañaupa Alvarez, Nilda. *Secrets of Spinning, Weaving, and Knitting.* Atglen, PA: Schiffer Publishing, 2017.

Callañaupa Alvarez, Nilda. *Weaving in the Peruvian Highlands: Dreaming Patterns, Weaving Memories.* Cusco, Peru: Centro de Textiles Tradicionales del Cusco, 2007.

Hoffman, Eric, and Karen Baum. *The Complete Alpaca Book.* Santa Cruz, CA: Bonny Doon Press, 2006.

Hough, Elisa. "The Alpaca Blessing Ceremony." Smithsonian Folklore Festival (website), July 3, 2015. https://festival.si.edu/blog/2015/alpaca-blessing-ceremony/.

Safley, Michael. *The Alpaca Shepherd.* Hillsboro, OR: Northwest Alpacas, 2005.